MUNDO CRUEL

MUNDO CRUEL
Stories

Luis Negrón

Translated by Suzanne Jill Levine

SEVEN STORIES PRESS

New York

"Faggotry is always subversive."

—Eduardo Alegría

"So then, a melodrama is a drama made by someone who doesn't know the difference, Miss?"

"Not exactly, but in a certain way it is a second-rate product."

—Manuel Puig, "A Melodramatic Destiny"

Seven Stories Press
140 Watts Street
New York, NY 10013
www.sevenstories.com

College professors may order examination copies of Seven Stories Press titles for a free six-month trial period. To order, visit sevenstories.com/textbook or send a fax on school letterhead to (212) 226-1411.

Book design by Jesse Heuer

Library of Congress Cataloging-in-Publication Data

Negrón, Luis, 1970-
  [Short stories. Selections. English]
  Mundo Cruel : stories / by Luis Negrón ; translated by Suzanne Jill Levine. -- A Seven Stories Press First edition.
     pages cm
  ISBN 978-1-60980-418-3 (pbk.)
  1. Santurce (San Juan, P.R.)--Fiction. I. Levine, Suzanne Jill, translator. II. Title.
  PQ7442.N46M8613 2013
  863'.7--dc23
                                2012046128

Printed in the United States

9 8 7 6 5 4 3 2 1

Contents

❧

THE CHOSEN ONE

Ever since I was little I've heard my mother tell the story, more than once, that when they presented me at church, barely forty days old, the preacher predicted that I would not be like other boys, that every step I took would be a step toward Jehovah. I grew up with the certainty of being anointed.

My brothers and father were opposed to this idea. Papi swore to my mother that they weren't bringing me up right, that all the church and religion was going to ruin me. My brothers, backed by Papi, never went to church. They made sure I had something to talk about in Bible class when we'd discuss Job and his trials. They'd hide my Bible and my neckties. They'd spray me with the hose minutes before the bus arrived to take Mami and me to worship. If I cried, Papi would make me fight them and would shout at me:

"Defend yourself like a man, goddamn it!"

I felt comfortable at church. They'd take me from town to town as a child preacher. The adults would ask my advice; the women would beg me for visions. One night during a vigil, I went out to the bathroom. The only light outside was the one on the toilet. When I entered, I heard a noise and as I approached the urinal stall I saw sister Paca's son doing brother Pabón's son from behind.

At that moment I had my first true revelation. My whole body was telling me that I wanted to be in the place where brother Pabón's son was. When they noticed me they got scared, but I was able to calm them down when I started to lower my pants. I wasn't able to touch them, though, because at that very same moment brother Samuel came in and caught us.

The news reached Papi through my brothers, who were eager for the beating that would follow. With the eyes of a Pharisee, while Mami turned up the volume on the radio that was playing the evangelical station, Papi grabbed my whole face with one hand and crushed it like a ball of paper in his fist. He took off his belt and whipped my back. When he saw that I wasn't crying, that I didn't make a peep, he whipped my face with the buckle until the little choir on the radio stopped singing. He left both of my eyes swollen and my nose broken. After the swelling went down my face was transformed. It looked like the faces of the saints in those little prayer cards my grandmother, the Catholic, kept in her house. For the other boys it was irresistible. They all wanted to be my boyfriend.

The preacher's son gave me an illustrated Bible on Valentine's Day. I liked to look at the pictures: Adam covered with a big fig leaf, ashamed to notice his private parts for the first time, and me with him; Lot's wife turned to salt, looking toward the burning city because you just had to; David's torso, strong and magnificent; Goliath's legs, with him being a giant and all, my imagination soared.

My father decided to go to church too to see if he could change me by force of prayer. He was tired of giving me beatings every time he caught me making out with a male cousin or walked in on me when I was modeling in front of the family mirror. He'd drag me out of the bathroom at the supermarket where I'd hook up with meat packers. He'd slap me hard or punch me with his clenched fist, and

I just took it. Beatings with leather belts, belt buckles, flip-flops, wooden switches from tamarind or gandules trees that my grandmother sent from Arroyo, or pulled off the lemon tree that we had in the yard. I hated the lemon tree. One time my brothers and I claimed we had seen the Virgin appear on top of it. The news upset Mami and, fearing that the house would be filled with Catholics, she cut it down and there were no more switches.

When I turned fifteen it was my turn to be baptized. I didn't let Mami buy my outfit at Barrio Obrero. I made her give me the money and I went to the mall instead. The clothes had to be white. I bought a pair of linen trousers and combined them with a white guayabera shirt and leather women's sandals that really looked like they were for men. Nobody would notice the difference.

I took the bus and felt happy when I saw the driver. "Thank you, Father," I said to the Almighty. We already knew each other. Every once in a while he called me and waited for me at Parada 20 to take me to a motel on Highway 1. I sat where he could see me through the rear view mirror and where I could see him perfectly. He told me, when I was about to get off, to go to the end of the route with him, that it was his last trip for the day. From there he took me to a motel in Caguas.

Since we got out early I decided to run by the house to leave the bag of clothes I bought before going to church, where there was a fritter sale going on to raise money. When I got home, there was the preacher's son. He had come to find out why I hadn't gone to church. Nobody was home and I invited him in while I took a bath. He came in, nervously. I took him to my room. He sat on my bed and I stripped naked in front of him to go into the bathroom. I let the water run before getting in so it could get hot. I hated cold water. When I got in, the preacher's son stripped naked and got in with me.

Afterward he went off to church and I stayed home. I called Mami to tell her I was staying home and to bring me fritters. Two and a diet coke. Mami said she'd be back much later since they had to take a sister to Humacao and that was far away. I went out on the balcony and started to smoke a cigarette.

I learned to smoke with a Christian singer who once played a show at my church. When I noticed him he was flirting with a group of young sisters, talking about the Word. I watched him from afar and noticed how he got distracted whenever he looked at me. He didn't take his eyes off me while he sang a Christian bachata and read a psalm. When the concert was over he greeted me with a trembling voice.

"Do you sing?" he asked.

"A little."

He invited me to join his choir. I gave him my number, but before that he spoke with my parents and told them that being in the choir was a good service, a special calling. The preacher agreed and my parents gave me permission.

I was on tour for a whole summer and all that summer we were lovers. He loved me in an obsessive way. When he'd light a cigarette he'd give me one and I've smoked ever since, secretly and all the time. He'd say the smoke made his voice hoarse and that that turned on the sisters. He'd tell me that when he crossed over to worldly music he was going to take me with him so we could live together. We'd make love every night and sometimes in the morning. But I got tired of my calling and went back home.

While I was finishing my cigarette sister Dalia's husband was walking by. He works in Acueductos and has strayed from the Word.

"That's bad for you," he said to me, and stopped, not before looking around on all sides. "Are you all alone?"

"Yes."

"You always seem so quiet and I'm surprised to see you smoking. Maybe you ain't such a little saint after all."

In Mami's room—to keep an eye out through the window—he pulled me by the hair and possessed me, salivating and telling me how delicious it was to do it with me. When we finished, sister Dalia's husband left. I lay down, picked up the Bible the preacher's son had given me, and read a psalm to put myself to sleep. The next day was my baptism.

Mami was furious when she saw the sandals before we started out for the baptism in the Yunque. "You look like a damn fag," she said to me. "You're not going anywhere dressed like that." I didn't change. She hit me in the face with the tambourine, she pulled my hair and kept slapping me but I didn't change. I was going to the baptism in that outfit. After she got tired of beating me, she said to me:

"You're the one they're going to call fag."

Once we got there, Mami grabbed her Bible and left me. I went over to sister Evelyn, who was in charge, and signed in. Then I walked toward a place a little farther away, where the church buses were parked. I sat on a rock, still swollen from Mami's beating. I looked at the sky and told God I needed to talk to him. God spoke to me with a voice that came down from heaven but that I felt right in my ear. "Thou art proud and of a mind that thou canst do whatever thou wouldst." "But Father," I said to him, "if I'm a chosen one and I can't do what I want, what's the point? Besides, forgive me, as you are God, but I remind you that I also have free will." He fell silent, but I listened to him think.

"It's up to you," he finally said. "Go thou with my blessing."

I was satisfied when the meeting ended. I had made my point. From the rock I saw one of the bus drivers sitting in his driver's seat, looking at me. He gestured for me to come over. I climbed into the bus and he had already pulled it out of his pants. We continued in the last row. I liked him because he talked dirty and, grabbing my face amid all those dirty words, he said he'd never seen anything like it. I left the bus in a sweat, dying for the baptism to start so I could cool myself off in the water.

I got in line and they gave me a candle. Papi, who had gone earlier to help the pastor set up, was with Mami. They watched from the riverbank with desperate looks on their faces. They wanted them to put me under the water already to see if the Holy Spirit would enter and change me. I was the third in line and soon it was my turn.

The pastor looked at me with that prophet-look he knew how to put on. I saw him look at me with anger and then his eyes saw my slutty face. Full of pleasure upon seeing me look at him that way, he revealed his rage to me. I saw his dark thick body through his damp white clothes. I saw the hairs on his wet arms, close to his skin. I saw that he saw that I saw what he saw. I saw through his white pants how inside his white cotton jockey shorts, he grew large. I saw the brothers on the shore fascinated with my beauty, looking at me. I saw Papi's face in the distance, looking at me look. This boy is a monster, his face said. I saw Mami look at my monstrosity in Papi's face. I turned my back on my father and my mother and looked again at that thing that was already curving over the preacher's thigh when he immersed me in the water.

The sound of the water pressed against my ears. Among the rocks there was a beer can. Some river shrimp clung to an old tennis shoe. I saw the preacher's feet in his blue rubber flip-flops. Then he took me out of the water and held me for a second in his arms. "You are clean," he said to me, and winked.

A while later, when they were taking photos of me with my parents, he announced that I would go back with him, alone to the church, because we had things to talk about. My parents gave me permission.

He couldn't wait until we got to a motel: he made me

touch him on the way there. I caressed it and looked at it (identical to his son's).

"I felt something divine," he confessed still exhausted on the bed. "You're a mystery to me."

He hugged me and cried. He took me in his arms like the day of his prophecy and told me that he loved me. I promised to love him forever and to go live with him in Orlando and to found a church there, but I didn't want him to take me home in his car. I asked him to leave me near the church. I wanted to be alone for a while and clear my head a little. And feel the cool night air on my face. And why not see besides if I might find some guy on the way home. Then I'd lie down, read a psalm, and fall straight to sleep.

THE VAMPIRE OF MOCA

⌘

Let's put this story in context. Santurce, Puerto Rico, once known as Cangrejos, meaning Crabs, but no longer. Santurce. Blocks and blocks full of doctor's offices and temples—Catholic, Evangelical, Mormon, Rosicrucian, Espiritista, Jewish, and yoga-ist, if that's what you call it. The stench of sewers 24/7. Unbearable heat. Reggaeton, old school salsa, boleros, bachatas, jukeboxes, pool halls, slot machines. Topless bars, Dominican bars, gay bars. Catholic schools, beauty schools, vocational schools, and schools where you get a professional degree in just one year and without much homework. Fabric stores, arts and crafts stores, no-prescription drugstores, barbershops and hair salons. But the mecca is the 7-Eleven, which is like saying Santurce's Plaza las Américas. That's where I met him.

I look out the window and in my mind I still see him coming. His loose, low-hanging jeans showing quite a bit of those boxer shorts that didn't fall off thanks to those beautiful buttocks guarding his back. His sneakers, always neat and clean, not a thread in his shoelaces out of place, not the slightest stain on the sides of his soles. His striped polo shirts, his silvery watchband dangling on his wrist: I sigh because that's all I can do. His place, the 7-Eleven, I tell myself.

Let's go to the beginning of the story because I'm in no mood for games. I have a house in Santurce, behind the old General Committee Headquarters of the Pro-Statehood Party. (I should explain that it's by pure chance that I live there since, like almost all the protagonists of Puerto Rican literature, I question the US presence.) At the rear of my house I rent out a studio. It's little, but very comfortable. A year ago I rented it out to a couple of lesbians. I'll admit this was a bit sudden on my part, since when I agreed to it the gay parade had just happened and I felt a sense of solidarity. Horrible mistake. Every Saturday, without fail, there was an endless line of women entering my house. They'd begin by turning on the barbecue and playing Ana Gabriel and Shakira, and then pay-per-view boxing, and finally, being folkloric like they were, they'd bring out the tambourines and cowbells to sing along to Lucecita's *plenas* CD. As soon as the lease was over I told them I needed the apartment empty. "No problem, man," one of them said to me, and they moved.

It was then that I made little signs announcing the apartment for rent. Naturally I stuck them in the gyms and near the pretty boy bars with the hope of renting out the studio and landing a hunk at the same time. And as the saying goes: "Be careful what you wish for; it might come true." That same night I got a call from a guy who worked at the 7-Eleven and was looking for an apartment. I liked his voice. It sounded real macho. No slouch myself, I went right over to Fernández Juncos to meet him. When I saw him I was almost struck dumb. He asked me how much the rent was and I managed to answer him as best I could after giving him a substantial discount. He asked me about the deposit and I told him to forget about it. I didn't give him the key right then and there because I didn't have a copy. We arranged to see each other the next day.

When I got out of there, Santurce was suddenly

transformed into the dream of every urban planner: an Eden with Adam standing behind the counter of a store that—like me after that day—never sleeps.

The next day I didn't go to work. With the help of a Dominican boy, who by the way was also a hunk, I devoted myself to cleaning and painting the studio. I put in an air conditioner, a television, and even an illegal connection to my cable TV, which costs me almost fifty bucks a month. I put new sheets in there and a radio Mami left behind when she went with my sister to Orlando. I mean, what didn't I do.

He arrived around 9:00 PM and when he went in and saw the place he said to me:

"Damn papi, this is nice. With AC and everything."

He took it right away and told me that if it was okay with me he'd move in the next day. And that's what he did.

The night of the move—two plastic bags full of clothes, a box filled with sneakers, and a videogame system—I made him a delicious dinner. The poor thing, he brought beers from work and a box of cigarettes for each of us. He told me that he came to the city because he couldn't find any work in Moca, his hometown, and that a guy he met in Isabela offered to pull some strings and get him a job in a store. The guy brought him home but then wanted to fuck and he—and I quote—"had respect for everyone but wasn't into that shit." I felt so embarrassed for the other guy that I blushed, but he immediately added, "Bro, no worries, I know not all of you are like that. You've done right by me and you're not gonna regret it." Good God, he saw right through me! But how could he not? I'd put curtains in the studio for him for heaven's sake. I excused myself at that point and went to my room thinking that it was time to develop a little self-respect and to stop acting like a '60s fag, that we were now in the twenty first century and love wasn't something you bought.

I was so alert to the silence coming from the studio I almost didn't fall asleep.

The next day, determined to stop all the tricks and shenanigans, I went over to bring the boy some breakfast, not to take him to bed, but to feed a human being. The night before I had said to myself, "Enough of this, going nuts for a man." I knocked on the metallic door and he opened right away. Good God. He was in boxer shorts that were all snug around his thighs and he had a hard-on. He had a bit of a beer belly from standing on that corner so much and drinking cold beers, adjusting his package every time a hot mami passed by. He had a tattoo of the name Yomaira crossing his chest and sticking out from his armpits were some blond hairs, which really turn me on. I forgot my plan, called in sick at work for the second day in a row, and invited him to the Plaza Mall to buy him whatever he needed.

And so the days passed. My friends in the bar gave me up for dead. Then la Carlos came by to visit. I was with the boy on the balcony when I see him park across the street. He gets out, opening the door and looking at the young hunk and looking at me says as fruity as she can be:

"Can I come in, or are you busy?"

The boy excused himself and the queen looked me up and down with a straight face and said to me: "Girl, what are you doing with that macho?"

La Carlos never changes, I thought and was happy to see him. We laughed our heads off that night and he convinced me to go with him to Tía María.

Tía María, my second home. And I say this honestly. I love that bar. The two pool tables, the jukebox playing Lissette, Lucecita, Yolandita, and la Lupe. I hadn't gone back there since the boy had moved into the studio. It was really good to see the usual queens, especially since I hadn't been there for a while. I felt like fresh meat and in that trade that was a plus. Everyone found me thinner.

And then a little macho hustler, a bit like my tenant, came by and la Carlos looks at me and says:

"And the kid? Does he fuck?"

I said no—real serious-like—that I had rented the apartment to him, that he was from Moca, that he had a daughter named Yomaira and was easygoing and a hard worker. I said besides that he didn't interest me as a man. La Carlos, who doesn't waste any time, interrupted me:

"So then, I have carte blanche, right?"

"I don't care..." I lied, shrugging my shoulders and feeling that icy sensation in my bones that we call "jealousy."

One night I was on double shift and when I get home I see, parked right in front of the house, Carlos's car. I go and peek in the studio and there was Carlos with the guy, eating pizza and smoking pot. Fucking queen, I thought, but I put on a serious face and said to the kid:

"Dude, I don't want any trouble with the neighbors. If you're going to smoke, fine, but with the door closed."

The motherfuckers laughed right in my face, high as kites. La Carlos hugged me around the neck and said:

"You jealous, papi? Look, he's yours, no worries, right, papi?"

"Course, man, sure. All yours," the kid said, humoring me.

Those words remained engraved in my brain like Bergman's movies: "All yours, papi, all yours." But "all yours" was that he was friends with la Carlos and they went everywhere together.

I did what everyone would have done: I called my ex, the one who cheated on me in Santo Domingo, so that he'd tell me that, after me, he never met anyone as special. That's why it's good to stay on good terms with one's exes, especially if they treated you bad.

Time passed and Santurce went back to being its usual paradise lost. The same calm from Monday to Wednesday and the same hyped enthusiasm of its publicized weekends. I took advantage of all this and went to the museums—MAC, MAPR, Bellas Artes—and to all the movies they were showing at the Fine Arts and the Metro, except the one with Mel Gibson, who I can't stand because he's homophobic.

I felt defeated. If there's one thing I am and have always been it's a sore loser. It makes me angry and even makes me feel invisible, incapable of entertaining any delusions. Now Carlos no longer even bothered to greet me when he'd come to the studio, and from my balcony I'd watch my Adam come and go looking more and more handsome and more and more distant. One night I had one too many beers at the bar and as two hustlers came over to offer me their eight and nine inches, respectively, I quickly came down from my high spirits. I always get depressed when a trick propositions me: I feel old, or what's worse, I feel I must look old and pathetic for these creatures to consider themselves objects of my desire. I said to myself "fuck this" and went home. Once there I saw la Carlos's Tercel and I went over to the studio and looked in the window. The kid and Carlos naked in the bed I had bought, with the air conditioner I had bought, and between the sheets I had bought. And that was the stud of studs, the big macho, I said to myself totally pissed, and suddenly the kid gets up and I step back from the window. After a short while I look again and when I see what I see I start to add up all my expenses and I realize that this little Adam of Moca owes me and plenty: Carlos was fucking him.

I sat on the balcony to laugh at myself and Carlos and all of us gays, eternal denizens of Santurce, who have polished these sidewalks like crabs back and forth and sideways looking for machos, watching out for machos, or simply drunk out of our minds, out late, arm in arm, laughing jubilantly at the cars passing, shouting at us: fags! And us, raising our arms up high like beauty queens, shouting back at them: cocksuckers! And off we go to oblivion, holding hands, swishing all along Ponce de León. And I laugh at Carlos, who spent so much gas, the poor thing, coming and going from Moca, buying pizza and fried rice, and bumming reefers in La Colectora. La Carlos, like me, was thinking "now this is a real man," and as far as I could tell he's the kind who'd bend over in bed. Not that it's bad that he gave him his ass; it's just that us chumps give anything to charm them and to put them on a pedestal: handsome, male, virile, and one 100 percent tops. And I say to myself: "When that big queen Carlos comes out I'll invite her to Junior's Bar 'cause tonight there are strippers and I changed twenty bucks into one dollar bills. 'Cause there's always more fish in the sea.

FOR GUAYAMA

Sammy:

First of all excuse my handwriting since I didn't bring my glasses. It's just that, nene, I'm going nuts with Guayama being sick and all, I mean I'm really losing it. That's why I've been looking for you, so you could pay me for the curtains because with this Guayama thing I'm low on cash. I know you depend on your customers to pay me, but Guayama is dying on me. The doctor told me I had to put her to sleep and, nene, I almost fainted. They even had to rouse me with ammonia on a cotton ball and everything because I got so dizzy. He knows about cases like this and was real nice. He made me tell him how I found her and I explained that taking a drive around the island I picked her up in the middle of the highway right after the Guayama toll booth, hence the name. Last night I left her in the doctor's office so she could rest, but tomorrow they're going to give her the injection. When I got home, it felt so empty and I felt so afraid of being alone that I said: no, I'm not going to lose her. I immediately got on the Internet and found a place out there where they can stuff her. They say they leave the hair as if she were alive. You know that beautiful coat Guayama has. That's why I need the dough. Call me, nene, I need the money.

Your friend,
Naldi

❦

Sammy:

It's the second time I've come to your house to leave you a note and I can't find you. And on top of that, here's the note I left you yesterday. Nene, come on, call me or come by the house because I need that money urgently. Not for me but for Guayama, the doctor is pressuring me because she's suffering too much. The people who do the embalming are ready to take her but I need the money to send her little body over. It's really expensive. I'm so desperate I called Héctor, who as you know I haven't spoken to for over a year ever since he called me a pimp right in front of my sister, to ask him to lend me the money to tide me over until you paid me. A lot of good it did me to humiliate myself: that queen told me I was crazy, that it's the sort of thing only sick people do, which is why he stopped talking to me in the first place, and twenty thousand other things I won't even mention. That's why I need the money urgently. Call me, please.

Your Friend,
Naldi

Sammy:

They put Guayama to sleep this morning. I felt, nene, like I can't even say. Total despair. You can't let too much time pass after death to send her, but the doctor insisted and we did it. I was there to make sure, like the people who dry them out recommend—they have a name for that but I don't remember—that they not add any chemicals with color so as not to damage the fur, since it looks nicer that way. I felt sad but since I know I'll have her with the money from you for the curtains, well I wasn't so affected by it. I wondered so much about where you were I didn't have to be sad. This work costs money. I've got her all wrapped up in the freezer at the bodega next door, since for the lady it's no problem as long as she gets her *cuartos*, as she says. No questions asked. But, imagine, today they sent me a DVD from the company and you should see people with their little dogs, playing with them like they're alive. I'm telling you I'm desperate but here are the other two notes I left you before. Nene, where are you? The neighbor said you're in Santo Domingo. Knowing you, I'm not surprised.

Naldi

❧

Sammy:

I see now that you really are in Santo Domingo. Your landlord just confirmed it for me. In fact, he told me exactly where you are. You'll see. I need that cash and if you read this note I'm in Santo Domingo, since you know I get free trips because my sister works for American.

Naldi

❧

Sammy:

As you can see from the stationary this note is on, I'm in your hotel but you're not in your chamber, as they say here. I need you to communicate with me ASAP. It's urgent. I'm also telling you I had to charge my room to your account. You can take it off the bill for the curtains. I'm desperate: Listen: when I mentioned your name here in the hotel, everyone understood what the situation was right away and they've showered me with propositions, but I can't put those on your bill. Besides, I'm in no mood for that with Guayama in that freezer in Santurce. I'm waiting for you.

Naldi

◈

Sammy:

I'm going to a town called Azua. After I told the girl at the counter what happened to me, she told me she had an uncle who stuffs animals. I'm going to see how they look because he has a showroom. If you come back, don't leave. Tell the people at the counter to connect you to Yasrelis's cell phone because we're here together. I'll come right back to the hotel today. Don't leave.

Naldi

◈

Sammy:

I'm back at the hotel and not even a note from you. They haven't heard from you. I'm leaving for Puerto Rico but I'm coming back in two days. I went to Azua and I liked the work the man does there. They can change the eyeballs to any color you want. They gave me a massage and I put it on your bill. I'll tell you about it later. This place is paradise. When I get to Puerto Rico a cousin of the guy who stuffs the animals is going to pick me up and he's going to come with me to the bodega to pick up Guayama and get her ready for the trip back. I think they cover her in some salts or something like that. Since I can't count on you for the money I'm going to pawn some jewelry mami had been saving in case I ever gave her a granddaughter. But what better granddaughter than Guayama? I'll be back here with the dog in two days. I'm so excited I can't wait to get there!

Naldi

∞

My dear "friend" Sammy:

I'm writing this letter from jail. Yeah, imprisoned like a criminal for having friends like you. If only you could see me. I'm all shaved and dressed up like a woman. I've got a husband they made me choose as soon as they figured out what the situation was. He couldn't be more common. It's humiliating. I need your help urgently. I gotta have the money for the curtains to pay my lawyer. The Azua thing was one big lie. As soon as I got to Puerto Rico the supposed cousin took Guayama to "get her ready." What he did was fill her with social security cards, birth certificates, and even passports. They caught me at the airport. It's a federal offense and I'm locked away for identity theft, smuggling documents, illegal appropriation, and God knows what else. Please, send the money to the lawyer because my sister won't even answer my calls. Guayama is in the freezer in the federal building. Now she's evidence. When the lawyer clears everything up and I'm free to go, they have to return her to me. I found out from a friend of my prison husband about a guy in Santurce who stuffs animals. I'm telling you, nene, practically next door. If only I'd known. Give me the money for the curtains, please, if not for me, at least do it for Guayama, please.

Naldi

LA EDWIN

Aló? . . . Girl, you're finally answering the damn cell phone! . . . If it weren't for La Jorge, I wouldn't know what's going on with you. Girl . . . So, you've moved all over Santurce . . . Yup, Jorge told me. Honey, you never learn. And it's not because nobody tells you. Look, it's not easy to live with relatives . . . What? The one that's playing? La Yola, girl, beautiful . . . C'mon girl we're talking about La Yola. She looks great. The queen that does her make-up deserves a prize all for herself . . . It's fabulous, I haven't stopped listening to it. No, girl, I'm not giving it to you. Because you move more than a circus. Like you owed child support. You disappear and then it's a pain in the ass to find you . . . No, honey, no, don't insist. It's better if you bring me a CD, and not one of those cheap ones from Pitusa that screw up the stereo, and I'll burn it for you. No, I don't have a CD to burn it. What do you think I am, a millionaire? . . . Yes, girl, this has the one that's a hit right now, but you've got to listen to another one that's amazing. La Yola lives every word of it.

Ahá! . . . Listen, changing the subject, did La Edwin call you? . . . Yes, Edwin. The one who thinks she's a man. Honey, the one from the support group . . . That's weird because that little queen is calling everybody . . . Yeah, her, that's the one . . . Oh, I didn't know they called her that. You're bad, girl, bad, bad . . . Well, she called me last night, drr-unk out of her mind . . . Saying that he felt all alone, that for him it was difficult to deal with this shit, meaning gayness . . . I let her go on . . . So she could get it out of her system. Wait a second, I'm getting another call . . . Aló, aló. Aló, aló. How weird, they hung up . . . The thing is a man left her . . . Yeah, girl, she got involved with one of those lefty fupistas who plant bombs and want the ROTC out of the university . . . Yeah, girl, since they can't liberate the motherland, they're just going to liberate themselves sexually. The thing is that La Edwin fell for this little "Che Guevara" and she's got it bad . . . Well, lots of poetry, lots of rallies together, and gallery openings, but when it comes to you-know-what the big machetero can't even use his machete in the name of the Cuban Revolution . . . No, girl. That's not the problem. It's that the guy was and is straight. You know, these young guys nowadays who think they're all bisexual . . . Girl! Step outside the bars and find out what's going on in the world! The fupista told him that he loved him but in another way, that it wasn't physical . . . That's it, platonic . . . Me? Well I said to her: "Girl, the time of the Greeks is long gone, OK?" The comrade, which is how they call each other, got himself a girl comrade . . . Ah!!! But with her he could connect sexually and then he told La Edwin that he wanted to continue with him on the emotional level . . . No, girl, nothing whatsoever. Not even that. But don't interrupt me, I'll lose my train of thought . . . Just wait a minute. That's when I said to him: "But honey, don't you fuck?" La Edwin, with all that studying and college, was doing what all us beginners do, suffer . . . Ay, girl, wait, I'm almost finished. Besides, you're always late and if one day you manage to get there on time, your boss will fire you for the hell of it . . . Don't interrupt! Where was I? Ahá . . . La Edwin kept hanging out with this man of the people and you can already imagine them, with the futon on the floor, burning incense, playing protest music, candles, T-shirts saying "Peace for Vieques," and writing poetry that doesn't rhyme. And how was La Edwin during all this? Fucking horny! And so the time passed and one day "Fidel" came home, gathered his things, and, girl, he left La Edwin for a rightwing Condado queen . . . Yes, girl, from Condado, and pro-statehood. I know!! They tell me La Edwin is so desperate that she even joined a gym. The poor thing told me the whole story on the verge of tears. The thing is I felt sad and mad at her at the same time and I said to her: "Girl, wake up, that's the way it is here. All queers are the same and you young ones want to change it all from one day to the next. Oh, bisexuality, oh, gay is a political identity, bulldykes and fags together all the time, but— get with it, honey—the world has been the world for a long time. And that's the way our world is." He didn't say a word. Strange because he'd always have a fit if people called him fag or girl. Then he said the part that bothered him the most was all that wasted energy . . . You know he talks that way. Waste? Waste? Girl, you don't know what waste is. But, I'm going to tell you. 1985. Seven. Not one, not two. Seven of my best friends including my lover— and no more and no less than eight months of being in a relationship—all died! Pum, pum, pum! One after the other. That, honey, is what I call a waste. So, girl, stop with all these experiments and nonsense and accept what you are. Queer. Q-U-E-E-R. You're a queer. 100% Pato. Queer as a queer duck. That's it. You know I tell it like it is. It's not for nothing that I'm still here. That is, me and la Yola, who's the only one who understands me . . . Yeah, I know. You gotta go. Call me, whenever . . . you damn bitch. No, you bring me the CD . . . I said no, girl. Bye.

༄

Aló? . . . Yo girl, tanto time! . . . Hey listen, did La Edwin call you? . . . The one who thinks he's so manly . . . Girl, yes, the baby of the group . . . How weird because he's been calling everybody . . .

JUNITO

❧

Yo, Junito. What's up? How are you, bro? . . . You know,
still hanging in there. Tomorrow I'm leaving, you know,
and this guy from La Colectora wants to buy my car and
I told him I couldn't give it to him until today, but he
wanted to check it out with his brother-in-law who's a
mechanic. On foot bro, how else? I'm going over to the
old lady's house to say good-bye and pick up some things
that she wants to send to my brother. It's been years since
I've taken one of these buses. Which is the one you take
to Parada 26? Ah, okay, thanks, it's seventy-five cents,
right? So tell me, man, what's up? Hell, it must be at
least a year since we talked. You know how it is. You fool
around too much, then you get married and you gotta

work and all that shit and, bro, there's no more time for anything. You better believe it, bro, that's why I'm out of here. It's all one big pain in the ass, and bringing up kids here, man, forget it. Yeah, two boys, the oldest is ten and the other one's nine . . . No way, she had the operation. I signed the consent. You know, things are tough and you can't keep having kids. We wanted a girl to have the little pair of 'em, you know? But instead we got another boy. It's okay, this way they can keep each other company, and, you know, defend each other . . .

No, not New York, no. We're going to Boston. I mean, it's above Boston. See my brother, Samuel, the oldest, the darker one, works in a factory there and they need people. He talked to the boss, and so that's where I'm going. I'm going ahead and later, once I score an apartment, I'll send for my wife and the boys. She's happy about it, the boys are the ones who are afraid because of English and all that, but you'll see, they'll learn fast . . . Me, I talk pollito chicken, you know, Spanglish, but I get by. If they talk to me slow I can follow, but when they start talking fast with all that guachulín, man, that's where they lose me. But, you know, in the factory there are lots of Latinos, besides everybody there speaks Spanish. Even in the stores, Samuel says.

And how about you, bro? Going to work? That's good. You studied and got a nice little job with the government, man, that's cool. Today those are the steadiest and you don't have to work yourself to death either . . . Yeah bro, nice and easy . . .

Junito, listen, sorry for saying this, but really, bro, if I was you I'd get the hell out of here. You know what I mean. People fuck with you here and they stick their nose in your business. I mean you, well educated and all, should blow this place. Man, I see things, and I know people, the ones who stand on corners and fuck with you. Junito this, Junito that. Just the day before yesterday, some jerk there at the rotary was talking shit about you and I said to him, bro, leave him alone, he hasn't done nothing to you, and then they started fucking with me, asking am I your husband, am I a trick, and me, man, I told them to go to hell and I went home real mad. Listen, leave people alone, if that's the way they are then fuck everybody else, as long as they treat me with respect, no problem. Besides, people got sons and you never know how they're going to turn out. That's why I'm telling you, Junito, leave here, man. Listen, the other day I was taking a walk around the Condado and, man, there were a lot of them there. I mean, there were some that were real built, you always notice something a little weird, but, man, there were guys who looked real good, you know. It looks like they all move to the same area and so it's easier for them to meet each other there. Yeah, you should go there.

But for Christ's sake, Junito, your mom made her life, you have to go out on your own. Besides, you have more brothers and they can share the work taking care of her. Don't screw yourself out of pity, man, you've got to live your own life.

I'm talking to you like this, man, because I'm sure of what I am. You know I don't like that whole scene, but I believe in live and let live. I mean, bro, things change; this is a different world. Do you get cable? They show lots of things, I mean, like, on Showtime they even kiss each other and everything.

One sec, Junito . . . Yo, Cristobal, hey baby, you know you're mine. Tomorrow's the day. No, my little brother is taking me to the airport . . . yeah, to Boston. No, man, to stay. Anyway, I'll come down later to say good-bye to the boys. Ok, see you there. Take care.

Nothing to be afraid of, we always fuck around like that . . . So yeah, man. Ah yeah, so they kiss and everything, and they look normal. If you saw them on the street you wouldn't think they belong to the other team.

It's just that on the outside there's more freedom for that kinda thing ... I think they even get married ... and have kids and everything.

I remember, bro, when we were kids, you know, I'd fuck with you a lot. 'Cause I was ignorant, man. Repeating the same shit everyone else said, but look, you ended up better than all of us and the ones that give you a hard time nowadays it's because they're jealous.

You wonder why I know so much about all this shit, man . . . Keep this to yourself, bro, I'm gonna tell you something I never told nobody ... See, my youngest boy, well, he's just like you. I'm telling you, ever since he was real little I'd watch him and watch him and, pam! You know what I mean ... At first that shit bothered me like crazy . . . he's my son and I know that people like him suffer a lot . . . I'm telling you, Junito, I'll kill the motherfucker who says anything to my son. One day the older kid started saying shit to him and I stopped him. This is your brother and you and him got the same blood. If I catch you calling him faggot again I'm going to break your face, you heard me? It's not easy, you know, you can't know for sure, but I got a hunch . . . His mother doesn't say nothing about it, we don't talk about it, but I know she knows.

One day I heard her talking with a sister of hers, the chubbiest of the three of them, who's married to the Holsum guy. That one . . . well that bitch told my wife that the little one's like that because she wanted to have a girl so bad when she was pregnant with him. That she should put him in Boy Scouts or karate and shit like that so he realizes he's a dude. And by the way, it's not that the kid acts like a girl or nothing like that; it's just that he's different. He's, I don't know how to put it . . . Well, that's why I'm going, man. Things are bad here but not that bad, you know, I mean you can get by here. But I want the kid to grow up in a real good place, so that if he really is gonna end up that way, well, he can at least be himself . . . It's not easy, Junito, but he's my son and I fucking love that little jerk. I'm leaving all this, man, because if not, I'm gonna go to jail because the first motherfucker that fucks with him I'm gonna kill the bastard, I swear.

I watch him go off to school, and I know he's thinking it, I just know it, man, he doesn't say nothing, but I know. I mean, you can't be overprotective with your children, but you gotta do what you can, know what I mean.

But maybe not . . . There are guys that seem that way and they aren't necessarily like that . . . .

Just a sec, Junito. Hey, what's up!? That's it! Tomorrow's the day. No, it's cool, I'll take the bus. The driver is pulling up right now. No, it's cool. Good luck!

That motherfucker who just said hello, I can't stand him, bro . . . Be careful with that one, he's a piece of shit that motherfucker . . . he cheats on his wife with guys who dress up like women at Parada 15 and he robs them blind . . . he beats them up and leaves them there . . . Everybody in the hood knows about it . . . abusive asshole and his poor wife's a fucking mess . . . And she was such a pretty girl . . . she even studied modeling and all that. Got involved with that shithead and fucked up her life . . . Me who never even tried to date her. I always said, that one, she's gonna marry some doctor or lawyer or someone like that. And look what happened: she got involved with that creep . . . One of those guys who cross-dresses tried to report him when he got beat up but he was the one who got screwed . . . the police even spit on him and all that when they took him to the police station . . . but that motherfucker will get his one of these days. I hope he runs into the wrong guy and gets what's coming to him, that'll put an end to his shit. I'm sorry, but people like that just piss me off, I can't stand the wife-beaters. I don't deny that sometimes I just look away when it comes to that shit but man, there's too many abusive shitheads out there.

Well, bro, here comes my bus. Take good care and go to the States or move to Condado . . . my wife will give you my address . . . if you decide to come up to Boston. And don't worry because if anyone knows I'm all man it's her . . . so get the address from her. So you can get away from all this.

BOTELLA

I told Caneca to leave the front door unlocked so when I got there I wouldn't have to shout from the street late at night, drunk so I could face the old man, who pays good but stinks of rum no matter how much he bathes. As usual he forgot and I had no choice but to shout Paco, his name is Paco but I call him Caneca, like a bottle of rum, even though he doesn't know. I shout Paco, Paco, and he hears me and I go in and he gives me food and a line of coke and sucks my cock and today I want him to make me come in his mouth—he makes me come like nobody else—so I wouldn't have to fuck him because I really didn't feel like fucking him that night, but I couldn't come and then he said to fuck him and I fucked him and

I said I was coming, but I wasn't, and I screamed and said he was mine and the old man came and I laughed because it was funny that he was such a faggot.

I went home but the door was bolted and there was a note on the door saying this time she meant it, that I was abusive and I should leave for good. I knocked on the door and her ma opened it and handed me a bag with my things and told me I couldn't come in, that the girl, her daughter, that is, my woman, didn't want to see me. I went with my bag to Caneca's house and shouted to him from the street but he didn't open up. I checked the door and it was open, I shouted again, but not a peep out of the old man.

I went straight to the fridge and drank some water because the coke was making me thirsty, and the way home was long and that's when I noticed it stank like shit, and I said, the old man is shitting and I went to the bathroom to tell him anybody could come in and kill you with the door open like that, and when I get there Caneca is sitting on the toilet with his tongue hanging out and a cord around his neck.

I was so scared I almost shat myself and I said fuck this, I'm outta here, and I left. But almost at the beach where I was going to see if I could find another old man or a gringo, I remember the fingerprints and go back to Caneca's. The door was the same and I take off a sock to erase the prints from the lock and wipe them off the fridge and the glass and the whole place, and almost the whole house and I wonder if fingerprints stick to hair because I grabbed Caneca by the hair when he was blowing me, but I don't think so and forget that and put the sock back on and go to the beach. The smell of shit stays with me and the whole way there I keep checking under my shoe to see if I stepped in a turd since the smell won't go away.

I go to the beach and there is not a soul and I find a newspaper and start reading and I remember the DNA in the old man's body and I go back to his house but buy bleach before I get there to pour it over Caneca and erase the DNA, which you erase with bleach.

I buy the bleach and the old lady who sells it to me looks at me like what does this guy want bleach for at this hour. I get to the old man's house and go in. First I pour bleach on his lips: I take off the sock, put it on like a glove and open his mouth to pour it inside. Then I push him with my leg so he falls into the bathtub and I throw more bleach on his butt which is all dirty. I open him wide and pour it inside until the bottle is empty and I turn on the shower and leave him there.

When I was about to go, I remember the empty bottle and go back to get it. I go out again and there's not a soul on the street. I go back home and apologize to her and she forgives me. She wants us to do it but between the coke and the scare I can't get it up and she tells me I smell like bleach, that I smell like a motel, and she kicks me out again and her ma gives me the bag with my things and I go for a walk thinking where can I leave the bag because I can't go back to the beach with the bag and I decide to go to the house of a professor I used to fuck but who doesn't want to anymore and I ring his doorbell.

He opens the door and says I smell like bleach and I make something up about being in a pool and ask him to let me take a bath and he lets me. He goes into the bathroom with me because he says I rob him every time he leaves me alone and it's true because I stole some CDs from him that no one wanted to buy from me because they were weird. I take a shower and he watches me but doesn't do anything and I wash my dick so that he notices it to see if he's up for it, but no. He gives me coffee and lets me lie down for a while but then he has to go to mass and wakes me up and tells me to leave. I pretend to forget the bag and leave it.

I go by Caneca's house and everything looks calm

from outside. No patrol cars or anything and I decide to go to the beach to see what's going on. On the beach I run into this guy who nobody goes with because he never has money and only pays with things. Bejuco, a thin tall guy who's eleven inches long, once got a television out of him but it was too much effort to sell it at the beach and he had to take it home, but he left it on the street halfway there because it weighed too much. The guy looked at me and offered me a cigarette and I went with him to kill a few hours.

He paid me with flip-flops and a shirt and I put them on and went to Caneca's house. Nothing, no police.

I thought I better call and say that someone died in such and such place. And I call and talk fast and the policewoman told me I have to call another precinct, that they don't have a patrol car and I hang up, but first I give them the address for Caneca's house again.

I go to the Metro theater and fall asleep because I don't like movies and the cold makes me sleepy but the movie ends and I buy another ticket and sleep again, but the movie is over and I have to leave the theater but it's already night and I go back to the beach and now there's more people.

They killed Paco, I'm told by Niebla, or Foggy as he's

called, another guy who hustles and knew the old man. I asked him what happened but he said he didn't know, that someone strangled him and then threw bleach all over him and I remembered that I left the empty bottle in the bag and head back to the professor's who was already back home.

The bag was on top of the table and he had opened it and asked me about the bleach and I said it was to clean myself afterwards, that it kills the AIDS and he tells me that they killed Paco and that they poured bleach all over him, and he asks me if I knew anything about that and I say no, I don't, that it was a coincidence.

He looked at me funny and then I strangled him with a cable so he wouldn't talk.

I took his wallet and it had about six hundred dollars and I said I'm buying a ticket and going to Mexico but at the airport they ask me if I have a passport and I say no, and I better buy one for Boston instead, a sister of mine lives there. But I remember that I didn't have my voter's ID on me and I go home and she gives it to me but forgives me, and I stay and miss the flight. In the middle of the night she wakes me up and asks me where I got those flip-flops and the shirt and she says she's not fucking stupid and kicks me out and I go to the airport and tell them I got there late but there's no flight until the next day, and then I go to the beach but it's full of police and not much business. From there I go to Río Piedras and cops everywhere. I run into Rabbit and he tells me two guys were killed and the police are looking for the guy who did it and that it was a hustler for sure. I ask him if he knows anybody at all who will take me in and he says I should go over to the beauty parlor guy because the beauty parlor guy had been around and fled when he saw all the police.

I take off for the beauty parlor guy's house and he lets me in and I fuck him. I fall asleep and he lets me sleep because he falls in love with guys and takes them in to live with him. The next day he made me a bath and made my breakfast and put out clothes for me so I'd be comfortable. I stayed in my underwear and I made him blow me after I ate. I stayed three days, but on the third day he had me fed up with the smell of hairspray and I went to the beach and met up with Botella.

His name isn't Botella, but I gave him that nickname because he always had a little bottle full of bleach on him to wash up after fucking and kill any weird shit. I remember Caneca who always said these marks are battle scars. Botella tells me that they're after him or suspect him because of the bleach and I tell him I'll give him a plane ticket so he can go to my sister's house because she was alone. And he said that's a good idea and we went to his house and from there to the airport and they tell us you can't change the name on the ticket but that's when I recognize a guy from the trade and I signal to him and he looks nervous but comes over and I explain and Botella explains that he's going to marry my sister. The guy tells us to talk to him in private.

We get something to eat. After a while I tell Botella to follow me and we go to the room, the guy's there and we're so grateful that we're already hard, but the guy says what he wants to see is us going at it and we go at it and I stick it up his ass cause that's what the guy wanted but I came too fast and he kinda wanted more but Botella came in my mouth and the guy changed my ticket and Botella left. He cried, the motherfucker. It wasn't me, he said, and he left.

I went off to the beach all worked up and because I'm staring off into space I step in some shit and it's from some goddamn junkie tecato and I go down to the edge of the water and wash the flip-flop but the smell doesn't go away and I sit down and wait for the flip-flop to air out in the sun, and I think of Caneca who had his flip-flops on when I threw him into the bathtub and I think of Botella, who's a fugitive from justice, and my sister who lives alone, and the girl who's always kicking me out but I know she'll take me in again.

I pick up the flip-flop and sniff it and it still smells like shit and I don't know why but I start crying like that motherfucker Botella.

So Many

OR

On How the Wagging Tongue Sometimes Can Cast a Spell

❧

Two worried—extremely worried—neighbors meet on opposite sides of the fence separating their respective homes and set to badmouthing everybody. One is a schoolteacher and she's well off. Her house has window bars, a solar water heater, a satellite antenna, and a two-car garage. The other lady is on her second marriage and this one is a keeper, God willing, and, if not and they break up or if he lets her down, she's not going to marry again: live with somebody yes, but no more marriages. She doesn't live as well as the teacher, but she makes an

61

effort to keep up appearances. The two are worried and, looking around constantly, they broadcast their alarm. Very alarmed and super worried, they unbosom themselves as best they can, and, when you think about it, they should be worried.

Worried Mother:

I'm sorry to say this, but that kid of Alta's is turning out to be a fag.

Worried Mother Too:

Isn't he though? I was saying the very same thing to my husband and he told me that we should make sure my Yanielito knows what's up and if that kid touches him or makes any moves, to give him a good punch and then come and tell us.

WM:

No, and they say it's not contagious! Kids get confused you know. I'm constantly saying "ick" or "fooey," "how disgusting," and "that's not right," but Alta acts like nothing's wrong. She doesn't do a thing to straighten him out.

WMT:

My husband says the same thing, that he'd grab him right away and give him a good hard smack. One day when we were shopping Yanielito suddenly wanted a stuffed animal and my husband hit him. He gave it to him good but usually he never lays a hand on them. I didn't say a word because after all he's the one who raised them and has more right than the sonofabitch real father of my kids who never even comes to see them. Every so often he warns me about it: Honey—he calls me honey—if I see anything weird going on with the kid, I'm going to fix him good.

WM:

The other day I was in Alta's house paying her for some products and the kid started crying because his dad turned off the soap opera on TV. If you could see him, girl, crying like a Magdalene and Alta says to her husband: "Take it easy with the boy, he hasn't done nothing to you, and if you're coming home all worked up, don't go taking it out on him." . . . and she goes and turns on the TV again. Goodness gracious, I feel sorry for that man. I bet she married him for the green card.

WMT:

No, those people are like that though.

WM:

But listen to this, I say to her: "Look, Alta, I'm sorry

to say this, but you're overprotective with that kid. He's a boy and dads have to be firm with them and treat them as if they were men. I know it's hard because you're the mom, but that kid of yours, he needs his father more than you right now. I'm sorry for saying this, Alta," I say to her, "but that kid of yours likes the soap operas way too much and you got to remember that he's a boy."

WMT:

And she got mad at you, right? Look, those people, they're hard workers and all that and it's true they have it hard in their country, but if you ask me they've got inferiority complexes. You can't say anything to them. That's why my husband can't stand them. He even wants to leave Santurce and he was born and raised here.

WM:

But listen to this. She says to me, the ingrate, "Don't worry, neighbor, that boy is just fine and he's being brought up without any delusions. And whoever doesn't like it," talking real loud so that the husband hears her, "it's enough that he has a Dominican mother and has to put up with all the prejudice here." And I said to her: "That's exactly why I'm telling you, because later on it's going to be worse for him."

WMT:

Well said. "Prejudice" my ass.

WM:

No, and she said thanks but she knew what she was doing, that she had a degree in counseling.

WMT:

Probably from Santo Domingo.

WM:

Nena, she got it here. Don't you know they're getting all the scholarships? But we're supposed to keep our mouths shut. I said to her: "Sorry, honey, if I offended you, but that wasn't my intention." That's her problem.

WMT:

Some psychologist, she only got to come here because her husband met her at a pool tournament over there and fell in love and sent for her. My husband tells me that at work there's one who says she doesn't get involved with married men because she wants to become a citizen. My husband gets all worked up about this because it's like he says: they come here and take over absolutely everything. Just go by Barrio Obrero, or Villa Palmeras, or Río Piedras. The farmers market is filled with Dominicans and you can count the people who are actually from here.

WM:

I'm telling you, girl, it really gets me, but that boy is going to suffer a whole lot because people are prejudiced. There was one working at the school as a librarian. We gathered signatures and complained to the school board until they got rid of him. He was cool and the students loved him, but, honey, there are a lot of lawsuits now and, you know, it's not good for the kids.

WMT:

No, it's just like my husband says. Now the fags seduce men in broad daylight, right on the street. He tells me that in the men's room in the Plaza Mall a guy was looking at him and looking right down at it and he punched him so the fag would respect, and then said to him: "Now go call the police 'cause I don't give a goddamn fuck." You know how he is.

WM:

They're filthy! Those pigs. Lord, forgive me, since I have sons, but I tell my students that it's not natural and even though some say no, I tell them they can get help for that. Yes, honey, in Caguas there's a church that sends them to Florida and they go to a camp there, and they come back nice and straight. The son of the lady who works for the Department of Public Works was sent to that camp and he already has a fiancée.

WMT:

Yeah, but you can still kinda tell.

WM:

And what do you say about my husband's brother? He's that way, that's why he lives in Philadelphia because people don't accept that here and when he comes we welcome him with the American and all, but he knows better and they stay in a hotel.

WMT:

My husband tells me about Margot's son and how he's like that too, and that everybody knows about it and they've seen him come out of one of those clubs with another guy. He tells me if he ever saw him on the street he wouldn't offer him a ride.

WM:

And the son of the people who own the store too, the fat one, who you could tell right away and is always reading *TV Guide* and with the poster telling people to vote for Victor, the one on *Who's Got Talent*? That one's a fag. And what do you think about the second son, the cute one? Him too. So handsome and macho-looking. But him too.

WMT:

Ay, Holy Mary Mother of God! So many, right? I'm tellin' you, my hair stands on end just thinking about it, and we haven't even mentioned the women.

WM:

Hush, girl! Don't say another word, the tongue is a witch.

Then there is silence. One woman, the WORRIED MOTHER, has to call Alta to tell her what the WORRIED MOTHER TOO said about her kid. The other one, the WORRIED MOTHER TOO, is going to call her husband on his phone to find out where he has gone all dressed up, because she's no fool. Each one goes home. We see them from a distance, and we can sense Santurce overflowing with that sweet threat that disturbs all the extremely worried and alarmed mothers. From what we can tell, it's no small matter.

THE GARDEN

Sharon took advantage of the fact that we were washing the dishes to tell me she had been thinking about the day when Willie, my lover, would no longer be with us.

"I can't stop thinking about him, Nestito. I always see him so down, getting worse and worse, as if he already sensed he's going to leave us soon."

It's true. He felt it ever since that evening he got the results back and put it in his pants pocket, accepting right away his reality. I met him that very night, at a lesbian party in Miramar. When we were introduced I tried to start a conversation with him but after a few minutes he seemed bored; he excused himself and went over to talk to some girls. He ignored me the whole night. He was blond, with muscular arms and a broad chest. A white boy (how I adored and still adore the white boys). I did what I could to attract his attention, laughing loud, talking in a loud voice, and I even passed around the hors d'oeuvres among the guests, and all he did was look at the plate and shake his head no. At one moment I sat alone and put on a sad face to see if he'd take pity on me, but nothing. Until it was time to go and I said I was leaving, as the last bus came at 11:00 PM. He said then:

"Which direction you going in?"

"Parada 20."

"I'll take you."

When we took the elevator down he told me he was positive. He said it as if insinuating that's why he had ignored me during the party. I thought twice but then said to him that wasn't a problem.

"I just found out today," he added, tapping his side pocket and I understood from that gesture that the paper with the results was there.

"What are you going to do?"

"Take you out to dinner," he said to me.

We've been together since that night. Two years, three months, and eleven days. Willie accuses me of being corny for making such a big deal about dates. He says

I'm more and more like Sharon, his sister, who lives with us in Santa Rita.

Sharon's worry had to do with the fact that Willie got it into his head that we should have a New Year's Eve party to bid farewell to 1989. He wanted a succulent dinner and good wine. He spent days ordering records for me to pick up at Parada 15. It didn't bother me to go. Before being with Willie I had lived near Sagrado, where I was studying biology I don't even know why, now. I felt at home in that neighborhood. In Río Piedras I felt afraid. The farmers market that Sharon loved so much terrified me. Too many crazy people on the streets, too many jewelry stores, too many loudspeakers repeating the same thing over and over again. Only in Willie's house did I feel comfortable.

"I want flowers," Willie ordered, again: "Calla lilies for him, gardenias for Sharon, and tulips for me. Bring blue candles for Yemayá, as I am her child, like you and Sharon are too . . ."

All three of us were Pisces. Willie said his rising sign was Leo, which was why he was the head of the family. Mine was Taurus, hence I was stubborn, and Sharon's was also Pisces, and that's why she was a total disaster. Sharon wrote down the menu, which, of course, Willie dictated from his bed.

Everything was ready for the New Year's Eve party. There were two nights to go. Willie had sent me to Tele-video, where Norma, the girl who always waited on him when he was still able to go, had the movie rentals ready that he had ordered by phone. There were two of them: a Mexican melodrama for Sharon and a musical for me, *The Sound of Music*, my favorite movie of all time. That and *Love Story*—which Willie hated because it was so corny.

Which was why Sharon shared her worry with me:

"He's being very accommodating, Nestito, and you know more than anybody how he likes to do things his way. All this is very strange. Willie is going, Nestito. Don't you leave me, you stay here, since I'll die soon too and leave you everything," she said in full recognition that what she was offering me was a great deal, but it was an honest proposal. "You're young and can get your life going again when Willie is gone, you know. And if you have a boy-friend, that's fine too."

We were in the patio, which Sharon and Willie called the "garden," as in the movies, attesting to their belonging to a family of academics. Their grandfathers and grand-mothers had taught at the university. Their parents had had the opportunity to study in Spain and had returned to teach at the Río Piedras campus. Sharon had never taught but worked for years as an assistant to visiting professors. She was fluent in four languages, besides Esperanto, that lingua franca dreamed up by some old Pole, which Willie disowned as a senseless invention of words that did not resonate with any lived experience whatsoever. Willie went to Columbia and returned with a PhD in art history, with a specialization in film studies. Their last name was legendary at the university, as significant as the bell tower itself. They lived in Santa Rita ever since it was built, way before it was divided into shacks with the sole purpose of making money.

The residence had high ceilings, three bathrooms, four bedrooms, and a garage where Sharon would hide to see her lover of more than twenty years.

"I don't know why they keep it a secret," Willie always wondered. "I don't know why she didn't marry him when Papá died, or why she receives him there."

Twenty years was a long time to someone like me who was barely twenty-three. It was a long time for anyone.

"They must have gotten used to it," I'd say, dying from curiosity to see the aforementioned, but Willie had made me promise that no way would I try to inquire into or find out the lover's identity, that that would be in bad taste, reminding me with this warning of my origins in low cost tract housing.

It was easy to know the nights when the date with the lover was about to take place in the garage. Sharon would suddenly transform herself, act nervously, try in vain to hide, with certain self-absorbed gestures, her anxiety over not yet having what she wanted. Around nine o'clock, if we were in the garden or in Willie's room, she would always excuse herself with the same phrase:

"I'm retiring for the night."

"She's going off to sin," Willie would say with a mocking tone, imitating a movie star's voice.

From the garage we'd hear the faint sound of a radio station that played only boleros. Later, after the visitor was gone, Sharon would sit in the garden and smoke, wrapped in a white robe that seemed silvery in the nocturnal light seeping into the patio. I went out to join her. She smiled at me.

"It's just a little sin," she said looking at the cigarette.

She invited me to stroll around the garden and I, deliberately, made us walk near the garage. Once there, I lied pretending that I had twisted my ankle and leaned against the garage wall.

"I'm hurt," I said to her as in a movie. "Please, Sharon,

could you go into the garage and bring out something I can lean on like a crutch."

At that point we heard Willie's voice calling to us from his room in the back of the house. I got scared and pretended to quickly recover also as in a movie. Sharon offered me her arm to lean on and said to me:

"Never ever go into that garage. Your life would be in danger."

Hers was not a common warning, like my sister saying, "I'm gonna kill you, you damn brat." The danger was something else, beyond her.

"Nestito," she said with her girlish nasal voice, "I'm going to tell you a secret."

My heart beat faster, anticipating the pleasure of hearing what she was going to say.

"I am the victim of a kidnapping. For the past twenty years a big shot in the underworld has been forcing me to meet with him in that garage. He's from the mafia," she admitted, her eyes open wide so that I would see on her face what a big deal it was.

"Kidnapped? For twenty years?" I asked, obviously in disbelief.

"Yes, even though you don't believe me. One night twenty years ago, without wanting to, I was his. And I say 'without wanting to' because I, really, wasn't myself. He was handsome, like Sydney Poitier, the black actor in the movies. Identical. At first I confused the two of them. One night he came here and we started talking. I said to him, after a while, let's go to the garage, and out of pure foolishness I surrendered to him. Obviously I told him that was the last time, but he threatened to tell Papá all about it and to ask for my hand in marriage. I had no choice but to accept when he told me he was in the hampa mafia. Even though he's not Chinese, he's from Haiti, but he knows Chinese. He teaches me. I'm going to learn it well so that you and I can talk without Willie finding out what we're saying. Nesti, don't say a word of this to anyone. Our lives are in danger."

I was speechless, but that was her way of explaining her reality. I felt bad for being indiscreet. Perhaps I had taken her too close to being exposed, and being as classy as she is she preferred to step forward on her own and expose herself directly. In her own way, is what I mean.

Willie called again. We went over to where he was.

"Later I'll tell you more. 'I love you so much' in Chinese is 'chon chuan' or 'chon chun.' Something like that," she said to me with convincing pronunciation.

The former living room, where there had once been a

piano upon which, according to Willie, Sharon used to massacre poor Chopin, we had equipped to avoid climbing stairs ever since he had gotten worse. We placed the bed facing the big window onto the garden, from where he could see the bougainvilleas. The room was lined with books. Willie was a voracious reader. He'd read Hesse the same as he would read Amy Tan. He didn't let me take them to the bookstores on Ponce de León to sell them and with that buy others that he wanted. There he was with his glasses on to read, with a book in his hands.

The face he had when I met him was submerged in a new face that I could only identify as his by his expressions. He still acted like the handsome being that he had been. He shouted to his sister:

"Sharon, go to the salon so that Quique can do your hair for New Year's Eve."

Sharon tried to protest, but Willie insisted.

"Let them make you look like Diana."

Sharon, as if by magic, was excited by the idea and left the room saying:

"Me, like Lady Di? That's crazy."

As if crazy were precisely the most brilliant thing in the world.

I lay down next to Willie. He had recently taken a

bath. He had changed with me ever since he became bedridden. For months he had ignored me as at the party where we had met. I wasn't me, I was part of a duo with Sharon. "You two this, you guys that." I looked closely at his body and passed my hand over his chest. His armpits were tender ground for little flowers. I hugged him gently. His bones felt fragile. Body, host. Orchard fed with alien nutrients. I sought his face, kissed the dry sores, brushed away an eyelash that rested on his cheek. I looked in his eyes and found, finally, after eight months and sixteen days, desire.

I move his body with care to be able to put my arms around his back. His mouth, dry, like sandpaper, began to kiss me in rhythm with my lips craving his. His arms, thin like branches of a feeble shrub, tried to hug me tight. He smelled of recently primed earth. I rubbed my nose against his chest sticky because of the patches. He squeezed my skin as if not to fall, but his yearning sustained him. The disposable diapers, stuck to us, sounded like the rustling of dead leaves. We looked at each other. We continued in silence, sure of ourselves, safe.

I stayed in the bed with him. I remembered the first time I came to his house, the two of us in the garden. He lit a roach and we smoked. He fascinated me, with his eloquence, speaking about philosophers and writers as if he knew them, with his natural, well deserved arrogance. After, naked in bed, him with a Virgin medallion on a chain around his neck, his breath heavy with marijuana.

He looked at his pants hanging over the chair and with a smile he said:

"I should be crying, and yet, I feel fine. You want to see how fine I feel?" he asked me leading my hand to his erection. It began to rain. I noticed he was getting goosebumps and I covered him with a blanket.

"Sharon says you're going to die because of the party."

"I'm going to ask you a favor, Nesti," he said, serious, in the same way his sister would. "Take care of Sharon. She wants to leave the house to you and she says that she'll even build an apartment for you," he was emphatic: "You know? Every single member of my family, absolutely all of them, were born under the sign of Pisces."

We watched the rain falling on the bougainvilleas. We fell asleep.

When I awoke I went to my bathroom and took a shower. I loved that sense of security I felt after making love with Willie. I wiped myself dry and smoked pot. I thought of Sharon's story and I smiled thinking that these people were my true family and that this moment of my life was going away with Willie. Everything was going to change. Afterward, with the high, the thought came to me that Willie had died. That he was lying dead in the bed. I imagined the police asking me the requisite questions and myself rambling, incoherent. I came out of the bathroom in my towel and went straight to the room. Willie was standing. He looked strong, healthy. He looked at me and said:

"That butt of yours works wonders."

We received Sharon in the garden. She looked radiant, and made faces coquettishly as she shook her newly done hair, retouched with blond streaks.

"You look absolutely gorgeous," Willie rejoiced.

Suddenly she came out of herself and saw that her brother, prostrate in bed for months, was sitting in the little garden chatting with her.

"Willie, what are you doing up? Nestito, what's Willie doing outside here?"

I made a sign that she should leave him be and she understood. She straightened up like a soldier, looked at her brother and said:

"Whatever you say, and if you want, I'll open a bottle of one of Papá's wines, since it's a lovely evening and a little wine doesn't do any harm."

She trembled when she served the wine. She was a Pisces: I recognized in her that ability to deal with difficult situations and lost causes. We drank without saying cheers: for them, toasting was to waste a true moment of communion, in which the toast was always a lack of imagination.

We ended up in Willie's room, the three of us on his adjustable bed, watching *The Sound of Music*. I heard Willie's breathing wane again, at peace with his real reality. I felt a tightness inside my chest as if a dog were biting me there. On previous nights, when his body weakened and yet persisted arching its spasms of release, heaving what it no longer had, even so, taking him in my arms, leaning on his frailty, was joyful. A true joy holding in bed, in my arms, this generous being who was so daring, so sensual. So cheeky, as his sister would say. I wanted to take him to movies to see two pictures in a row as we used to do in the beginning. I wanted to take him to my house in Arroyo so that he could understand why I was such a hick. So that my parents would know that he was a professor, from a good family. So that we could go over to Guayama to the house of the poet Palés Matos, have an ice cream at the Chinese ice cream parlor, see a movie at the Calimano Theater.

On the TV, the von Trapp family was saying goodbye with a song.

Willie had left everything prepared for his funeral. He would be cremated and his ashes cast into the garden of his house in Río Piedras, near the bougainvilleas. It was a quiet ceremony: the friends who introduced us that night of the party, a Buddhist monk Willie suggested for his funeral one night high on marijuana and which Sharon took seriously; she, myself, and a gentleman who was introduced to me as an old friend of the family. He was black, tall, and strong and had a smile similar to Sydney Poitier's, and he gave me his condolences. Willie never got to see him, or to hear the end of the story.

Mundo Cruel

Ever since early that morning José A. and Pachi, the most fabulous and spectacular boys in the bar, had an ominous foreboding. José A., indisputable leader of the duo, woke up startled. He had dreamed that he was in Boccaccio, a gay bar in Hato Rey with an outdated 1980s dance floor. According to Pachi, the only people who went there were living room hairdressers, male nurses, civil servants, and, horrors of horrors, bulldykes. He not only dreamed that he was there, but that in the nightmare he was wearing white jeans and his hair was slicked down with shiny hairspray. Poor José A. To make himself feel better he went into the bathroom and vomited. That always calmed his nerves and made him look slim.

Pachi, also a spectacular boy and one who always showed up with a here-I-am look that everyone immediately noticed, had an anxious moment the night before. He was suddenly awakened by the awful idea that they might have cut off his cell phone service and, although he could still make phone calls, he needed to make sure he could receive them. He didn't think about it twice. He went downstairs to call from the public telephone. Without a minute to lose he quickly tried on six T-shirts and four different pants to see how they fit. He rubbed gel into his hair, shaved his legs a bit, and left thinking that if they had cut off his service it was because some envious queen who worked at the cell phone company was messing with him. But when he got to the public phone, he called his number and saw the lights on his Blackberry blink. "Hello," he said to himself and when he heard his own voice answering him, he was concerned that he sounded so faggy. Well, at least it was activated, imagine how embarrassing if it hadn't been. Even so, however, as he walked along Ashford looking at his reflection in store windows, that foreboding stuck in his chest. It wasn't going away. My God, what was it? He wondered anxiously.

Of course he wouldn't mention a thing to José A. The

word "foreboding" could reveal a past put away and buried; he had a spiritist aunt in Carolina, not in fancy Isla Verde, but right smack in rundown "Country Club" territory. Carolina is like saying Loiza—a negro shanty town—and if that got around he'd be sunk forever.

Both met up at the gym in the morning and went at the weights so much that they came out almost stiff. During their breakfast of Gatorade with PowerBars they witnessed something which left them dumbfounded: Gabriel Solá Cohen, the head of Ambience Consultants, who owned the only lavender Audi in Puerto Rico and possessed such good genes that he had an almost made-to-order body, was eating no more and no less than fried eggs with white toast. They were so disappointed. If fabulous people put scratches like that on such a fabulous and spectacular soundtrack, if they had such habits, the world such as they knew it was about to end.

And so it was. The whole thing had been so unpleasant that José A. called his studio and asked his assistant to cancel all his appointments and engagements, as he was unwell: "I'm feeling awful," he said. The dream of the white jeans and the smell of fried eggs spoiled his mood. He looked at his watch and saw that it was noon, exactly twelve more hours before going to the bar. Better to concentrate on what he was going to wear.

Pachi, despite the upset, had no choice but to go to his office. The chief executive had called everyone to a meeting. Not only those in charge of accounts or management like himself, but everyone who was on the payroll. "Every man and every woman," read the email. The CEO himself opened the meeting saying, now listen carefully, this is a special day, since in tune with the new times and for the benefit of the business, its collaborators, male and female, he had invited some young leaders from who knows where, who were coming to talk about homophobia in the workplace.

Pachi was horror-struck when he saw these specimens, as one couldn't call them anything else. He had already seen them in the bar in their flip-flops and with their big baskets handing out condoms and leaflets for protests that nobody would attend. Here they were with their hair bleached, burnt from all the sun they got during those marches. Pachi had no choice but to repeat what was already his mantra: how ridiculous!

At the end of the presentation there were sixteen who came out of the closet, including Mundo, the janitor who said out loud for everyone to hear that he was a passive bisexual.

Everyone acted as if nothing special was happening. Nobody protested this absurd spectacle. But if there was something that he and his friend José A. were clear about, it was that faggotry wasn't something one broadcasted from the rooftops. When he realized they were all looking at him, he withdrew without offering any excuse. He went into his office, picked up his attaché case and his gym bag, smoothed his hair, put on perfume, and almost ran out the door.

Now in his Land Rover he turned on the radio and on all the stations, even the religious ones, there was an appeal to put an end to homophobia. What's more: right at the center of Ponce de León they were putting up a billboard with the photo of a couple of lesbians with two little black girls which said: There's no room for hate in the warmth of the home; let us live in diversity.

Pachi looked at it alarmed and saw a policeman in drag and not a single person seemed bothered. He saw a couple of young boys holding hands and nobody took the slightest notice. He was overcome by panic.

Pachi started crying when his cell phone rang, to his relief and consolation—how badly he needed it, after such a morning—after almost twelve hours without a phone call. It was José A. telling him to come to his house after work to get ready for the bar. Pachi, drowning in tears, could only murmur yes.

After going around the block six times, he managed to find a parking space, and pressed the intercom to request access from his friend. Trembling and sobbing he told José A. what was happening in the world. José A. hadn't noticed anything because he had spent the whole day giving himself a facial, a Swedish fruit mask. Following the directions for the facial, he hadn't been able to get up, not even to vomit, although at one moment he thought that the fruit in the mask could make him fat.

So what his friend told him seemed totally preposterous and he tried to comfort him, telling him not to worry, that that night they were going to the bar and that surely homophobia would be intact there. Succeeding in calming down his friend a little so that he could deal with this minor crisis, José A. went to his bathroom and vomited.

Stressful times, he had read in *Gay Style*, made fat accumulate in the body and, upon remembering this, he put his finger in again so as not to leave anything. During the next six hours they dressed and dolled themselves up so much that when they left for the bar at a quarter to twelve they seemed made of rubber and worthy of a show window in the Plaza Mall.

They were on their way to the bar in Pachi's Land Rover with the *Gay Ibiza VIP Club Music Collection* on the stereo concealing their anxiety that the bar too might be affected. But almost at the entrance to the formerly exclusive (men pay ten, women thirty, get my drift?) and super "in" bar, they saw the first sign that the world, their world, was going straight to hell. Six lesbian couples, with their cell phones on their belts, were entering. Alarmed and almost complaining they asked the bouncer in disgust, "Is this women's night?" The bouncer said no.

They entered as if thinking twice before doing so, but without slowing down and with their noses turned up, they went over to a corner to see whom they should ignore. There weren't as many people as usual, but the worst part was that almost all of them were dressed casual, not to say like ragpickers.

At that moment the music stopped and the DJ announced that everyone should go out on the street, as the city had declared the first Thursday of each month "Gay Nights in Santurce." Everyone went out on the avenue. José A. and Pachi went outside with a disgusted look on their faces and with their hands up high so as to not touch so many sweaty and dirty persons.

A section of Ponce de León was blocked off. An enormous commotion was growing, people talking, laughing, and dancing. Some Dominican women had even improvised a stand to sell fried food. José A. and Pachi went to a corner and there they encountered some activists, furious because no one had given them any credit for putting an end to homophobia. They should make an announcement, they said, to thank us.

At that moment, amid the dancing crowd, Pachi saw the sweet love of his youth, Papote, the fireman's son. He came toward Pachi with the same beautiful smile that led him to love him when they were in high school.

Papote, with gray hairs and the extra weight that the straight life causes, grabbed him by the hands and said to him: "Babe, come with me, I came out of the closet and came here to find you."

He gave the keys to his SUV to José A. so as not to leave him stranded, and before he knew it he was dancing a bachata right on Ponce de León with the man of his life. With one eye he saw the disgust on the face of his friend José A., but with the other he saw Papote's full lips. Even with his ghetto mustache and all, he gave him a kiss, and said, surrendering to come what may:

"Papito, I'll go with you to the ends of the earth, but

first take me to a restaurant for a plate of rice and beans because I've been hungry for the last twenty years.

And they left.

◇◈◇

José A. cried out of pure rage, not over Pachi, since deep down he knew his shortcomings, but because the clothes he wore had cost him a lot and it wasn't for going slumming like that. He turned up his nose, stopped behind the car to vomit the smell of fried food, and got in the car.

At that moment he promised himself that the next day he would sell everything and go to Miami. Since he, José Alfonso Lapís, of the Ponce Lapís family, didn't mix in with riffraff, and never would he live without decorum. Never!

*A Maritza Espinal, Gabriel Espinal,
and Suzanne Jill Levine, gracias.*

About the Author

LUIS NEGRÓN was born in the city of Guayama, Puerto Rico, in 1970. He is coeditor of *Los otros cuerpos*, an anthology of queer writing from Puerto Rico and the Puerto Rican diaspora. The original Spanish language edition of *Mundo Cruel*, first published in Puerto Rico in 2010 by La Secta de Los Perros, then by Libros AC in subsequent editions, is now in its third printing. It has never before appeared in English. Negrón lives in Santurce, Puerto Rico.

About the Translator

SUZANNE JILL LEVINE's many translations include the works of Guillermo Cabrera Infante and Manuel Puig. She is the editor of Penguin Classics Jorge Luis Borges series and author of *The Subversive Scribe: Translating Latin American Fiction*. She is the winner of the 2012 PEN Center USA Literary Award for her translation of José Donoso's *The Lizard's Tale*.

ABOUT SEVEN STORIES PRESS

SEVEN STORIES PRESS is an independent book publisher based in New York City. We publish works of the imagination by such writers as Nelson Algren, Russell Banks, Octavia E. Butler, Ani DiFranco, Assia Djebar, Ariel Dorfman, Coco Fusco, Barry Gifford, Martha Long, Luis Negrón, Hwang Sok-yong, Lee Stringer, and Kurt Vonnegut, to name a few, together with political titles by voices of conscience, including Subhankar Banerjee, the Boston Women's Health Collective, Noam Chomsky, Angela Y. Davis, Human Rights Watch, Derrick Jensen, Ralph Nader, Loretta Napoleoni, Gary Null, Greg Palast, Project Censored, Barbara Seaman, Alice Walker, Gary Webb, and Howard Zinn, among many others. Seven Stories Press believes publishers have a special responsibility to defend free speech and human rights, and to celebrate the gifts of the human imagination, wherever we can. In 2012 we launched Triangle Square *books for young readers* with strong social justice and narrative components, telling personal stories of courage and commitment. For additional information, visit www.sevenstories.com.